-the-
PIRATE KIDS

A Bad Day at Pirate School

BY Johanna Gohmann
ILLUSTRATED BY Jessika von Innerebner

Calico Kid
An Imprint of Magic Wagon
abdopublishing.com

For Fabian - I hope you only have great days at school! But if you ever have a bad day, just remember how much Mommy loves you. —JG

To CA who always helps me see the good in any bad day. —JV

abdopublishing.com

Published by Magic Wagon, a division of ABDO, PO Box 398166, Minneapolis, Minnesota 55439. Copyright © 2018 by Abdo Consulting Group, Inc. International copyrights reserved in all countries. No part of this book may be reproduced in any form without written permission from the publisher. Calico Kid™ is a trademark and logo of Magic Wagon.

Printed in the United States of America, North Mankato, Minnesota.
082017
012018

Written by Johanna Gohmann
Illustrated by Jessika von Innerebner
Edited by Heidi M.D. Elston
Art Directed by Candice Keimig

Publisher's Cataloging-in-Publication Data

Names: Gohmann, Johanna, author. | von Innerebner, Jessika, illustrator.

Title: A bad day at pirate school / by Johanna Gohmann; illustrated by Jessika von Innerebner.

Description: Minneapolis, Minnesota : Magic Wagon, 2018. | Series: The pirate kids

Summary: One day, Piper has a very bad day at pirate school. She can't find her silver eye patch. She drops her lunch overboard. She falls down in wooden leg practice. Piper can't wait for the day to be over! But when their teacher loses his golden compass, Piper is the one who finds it.

Identifiers: LCCN 2017946447 | ISBN 9781532130380 (lib.bdg.) | ISBN 9781532130984 (ebook) | ISBN 9781532131288 (Read-to-me ebook)

Subjects: LCSH: Pirates--Fiction--Juvenile fiction. | School--Juvenile fiction. | Fortune--Juvenile fiction. | Buried treasure--Juvenile fiction.

Classification: DDC [E]--dc23

LC record available at https://lccn.loc.gov/2017946447

Table of Contents

Chapter #1
A Stumbling Start

"Argh, Piper! Time to hurry. You'll be late for pirate school," Piper's mom calls to her.

"I can't find my silver eye patch," Piper shouts back.

5

"Just choose another one, honey," her mom says. "Captain Sharktooth is waiting."

Piper sighs, then grabs one of her old, black eye patches. She climbs up the ladder to the main deck.

"Hurry up, slowpoke!" Percy shouts from their teacher's boat.

Piper hurries to catch up. Just then, she hears another, more squawky voice from above, "Hurry up, slowpoke!"

Piper looks up. Poppy the parrot is perched on one of the ship's masts. Piper smiles at the silly bird.

"Hey, wait a minute." Piper sees something shiny gripped in Poppy's claws. It's her silver eye patch!

"Argh, Piper, you best scuttle aboard now, lassie," her teacher Captain Sharktooth calls from his boat.

"But Poppy has my silver eye patch!" she calls back to him.

"Ah, yes. Parrots love shiny things, matey. I'm sure you can get it back from her later. Hurry along now," Captain Sharktooth says.

"Shiny!" Poppy squawks.

Piper gives a sigh then scurries across the gangplank. Halfway there, she trips, and her lunch bag falls into the ocean.

"My sandwich!" she cries.

"Do sharks like peanut butter and jelly, Captain?" she hears Percy ask.

"That's a good question," Captain Sharktooth says. "Maybe we can find the answer in the pirate library. Come along, Piper, I have some leftover pirate stew you can have for lunch."

They climb below deck.

Piper watches her lunch sink into the sea. Her day isn't off to a very good start.

Chapter #2
Scallywag!

Piper and Percy sit at the long table
in Captain Sharktooth's classroom.

"Yo ho ho, shiver me timbers!"
Captain Sharktooth smiles at them,
showing off his gold front tooth.

"Yo ho ho, shiver me timbers, Captain!" the children call back.

"Today we're going to have our first lesson on how to read a treasure map. You'll each get a chance to use my golden compass."

Captain Sharktooth holds up his compass. It sparkles in the light.

"Oooh!" Piper and Percy exclaim.

OOOH!

"But first, it's time for wooden leg practice," Captain Sharktooth says.

"Oh no," Percy says. He slumps forward onto the table. "I'm terrible at wooden leg walking!"

"Well, that's why it's called practice. Right, Piper?" Captain Sharktooth says.

"Yep," Piper says. "I'll go first."

Piper hops out of her chair. She bends her knee and carefully attaches the wooden leg to her kneecap.

Suddenly, Poppy the parrot flies through a classroom window.

"Well, look who decided to join us," Captain Sharktooth says.

"I hope she didn't drop my silver eye patch into the ocean," Piper frowns.

"Yeah, you've already dropped enough in the ocean today!" Percy giggles.

"Oh hush, you scallywag!" she shoots back.

Poppy squawks and flies back out of the room.

Chapter #3
Where Did It Go?

"Alright now, children. No name-calling." Captain Sharktooth frowns. "Let's focus, please. Come on, Piper. Show us those wooden leg skills of yours!"

"Yes, sir," Piper says. "This is how you do it, brother!"

Piper carefully balances on the wooden leg. Then she does a quick run across the classroom. Suddenly, the boat rocks, and she tumbles to the floor.

"Ouch!" Piper cries. She can hear Percy covering a giggle.

"You okay, matey?" Captain Sharktooth helps her up.

"Yes." Piper pouts. She's never fallen in wooden leg practice before.

"Don't worry, lass. Remember, it's called practice." Captain Sharktooth flashes his golden-toothed grin at her.

Piper takes off the wooden leg and slouches back to her seat. She can't wait for this day to be over!

Percy gets up and has his turn with the wooden leg. He is very wobbly and slow, but he doesn't fall down.

"Now me freebooters, it's time for treasure map class!" Captain Sharktooth claps his hands.

"Wait, what's a freebooter?" Percy asks.

"Why, that's you!" Captain Sharktooth says. "Freebooter is a another name for pirate."

"Ah, cool!" Percy smiles.
.

"Now, where did I put my golden compass?"

Captain Sharktooth begins to pull things out of his coat pockets.

He pulls out a brass fishing hook. He pulls out a knotted bit of rope. And he pulls out a big, rusty key. But there's no sign of his compass.

"Blimey!" Captain Sharktooth says. "I thought I put it right here on the desk. I guess our very first treasure hunt will be to find my golden compass!"

Chapter #4
Piper Remembers

Captain Sharktooth, Piper, and Percy search all over the boat for the compass.

They look under tables. They look beneath old maps. They even look in Captain Sharktooth's refrigerator!

"Argh, nothing in there but pirate stew, I'm afraid." Captain Sharktooth sighs and scratches his head.

"I'm kind of hungry," Percy says. "Is it time for lunch yet?"

"Percy, we need to find the compass first," Piper says.

"But we've looked everywhere. I'm ready to give up," Percy grumbles.

"Captain Sharktooth, are you sure you put the compass back on the desk?" Piper asks him.

Captain Sharktooth tips his head to one side, trying to think. As he does, his earrings shimmer in the light.

Suddenly, Piper remembers something. "We need to find Poppy!"

Piper races up the ladder. Captain Sharktooth and Percy quickly follow.

"Aha! I knew it," she shouts.

There in Poppy's claws is Captain Sharktooth's golden compass.

"Yo ho ho, well done, Piper!" Captain Sharktooth says. "Now, that is what I call some clever treasure hunting."

"Well done, Sis!" Percy gives her a high five.

"Thanks." Piper grins. "Parrots love shiny things. Maybe I'm not such a bad freebooter after all!"

Captain Sharktooth smiles at her. His golden tooth flashes in the sunlight.

"Shiny!" Poppy squawks.

"Careful, Captain!" Piper says. "Poppy might try to take your tooth next!"

Together, the three laugh. Piper's bad pirate day suddenly doesn't feel so bad anymore!

SHINY!